Millie, Daisy, and the Scary Storm

Read all the books in the Life in the Doghouse series!

Elmer and the Talent Show

Moose and the Smelly Sneakers

Millie, Daisy, and the Scary Storm

Coming soon:

Finn and the Feline Frenemy

LIFE IN THE DOGHOUSE

Millie, Daisy, and the Scary Storm

DANNY ROBERTSHAW & RON DANTA

Written by Crystal Velasquez • Illustrated by Laura Catrinella

ALADDIN New York London Toronto Sydney New Delhi

🧞 ALADDIN

An imprint of Simon & Schuster Children's Publishing Division
1230 Avenue of the Americas, New York, New York 10020
First Aladdin paperback edition July 2022
Text copyright © 2022 by Danny Robertshaw and Ron Danta
Illustrations copyright © 2022 by Laura Catrinella
Photographs on pages 109, 113–114 by Danny Robertshaw and Ron Danta
Also available in an Aladdin hardcover edition.
All rights reserved, including the right of reproduction in whole or in part in any form.
ALADDIN and related logo are registered trademarks of Simon & Schuster, Inc.
For information about special discounts for bulk purchases, please contact
Simon & Schuster Special Sales at 1-866-506-1949 or business@simonandschuster.com.
The Simon & Schuster Speakers Bureau can bring authors to your live event. For more information or to book an event contact the Simon & Schuster Speakers Bureau at 1-866-248-3049 or visit our website at www.simonspeakers.com.
Designed by Tiara Iandiorio
The illustrations for this book were rendered digitally.
The text of this book was set in Museo Slab.
Manufactured in the United States of America 0622 OFF
10 9 8 7 6 5 4 3 2 1
Library of Congress Cataloging-in-Publication Data
Names: Velasquez, Crystal, author. | Robertshaw, Danny, author. | Danta, Ron, author. | Catrinella, Laura, illustrator.
Title: Millie, Daisy, and the scary storm / Danny Robertshaw & Ron Danta ; written by Crystal Velasquez ; illustrated by Laura Catrinella.
Description: First Aladdin paperback edition. | New York : Aladdin, 2022. | Series: Life in the doghouse | Audience: Ages 7 to 10. | Summary: Best friends Millie and Daisy worry about being separated during a dog adoption event.
Identifiers: LCCN 2022009814 (print) | LCCN 2022009815 (ebook) | ISBN 9781534482678 (hardcover) | ISBN 9781534482685 (pbk) | ISBN 9781534482692 (ebook)
Subjects: CYAC: Dogs—Fiction. | Dog adoption—Fiction. | Best friends—Fiction. | Friendship—Fiction. | LCGFT: Animal fiction.
Classification: LCC PZ7.V4877 Mi 2022 (print) | LCC PZ7.V4877 (ebook) | DDC [Fic]—dc23
LC record available at https://lccn.loc.gov/2022009814
LC ebook record available at https://lccn.loc.gov/2022009815

To Karen Odom, who, from the day she stepped in,

has never stepped out. We love you.

—Danny and Ron

OUTSIDE THE COZY brick house that was Danny & Ron's Rescue, a storm was raging. At least that's what it sounded like to Daisy. She had hidden underneath a blanket the minute the dark clouds rolled in, and now she was too scared to do any more than peek out.

"Aw, come on, Daisy. It's not *that* bad," said Millie. "It's just a little rain. See for yourself."

"No thank you. I'm fine right here."

Millie, Daisy's best friend in the whole world, sat right by the porch door, panting happily as she looked out at the drops of water falling into the yard.

She's so brave! thought Daisy. She couldn't figure out why Millie wasn't as scared of rainstorms as she was. After all, a terrible storm had once taken away their home. Rain had fallen for days, flooding the streets of their Louisiana town. If it hadn't been for the courageous people who came by in a boat to rescue Daisy and Millie from their porch, she wasn't sure what they would have done. Eventually Danny Robertshaw and his partner, Ron Danta, took them both into their home in South Carolina. For months afterward, any time a thunderstorm came through, Daisy would run to hide under the bed, and Millie would have to find her and convince her to come out.

To help Daisy face her fears, Ron hired a special trainer—Eileen Clark. Eileen had helped figure out what triggered Daisy's fears and taught her better ways to react when she felt afraid. It had worked . . . mostly. Over time Daisy had gotten a lot better. She stopped hiding under the bed, but she still didn't like rainstorms.

She curled into a tight ball now and squeezed her eyes shut. But soon she felt a tug at the edge of her blanket. Daisy opened her eyes to find Millie gazing down at her kindly.

"I know you're scared," said Millie. "But I promise there's nothing to be afraid of. Have I ever lied to you?"

"No," Daisy said.

"That's right. And I never will. Come look at the rain with me. You might even think it's pretty if you give it a chance."

"I don't know . . . ," Daisy said timidly. "What if the storm gets worse?"

"Well, then I'll be right by your side, and we'll keep each other safe. Deal?"

Daisy thought about it for a while. She did feel safer any time Millie was around. And if her friend wanted a little company, that was the least she could do.

"Okay," she said. "But if I see one strike of lightning—"

"You can come right back here and hide under the blanket," finished Millie.

Slowly, Daisy untangled herself from the

yellow knit blanket and followed Millie to the porch door where they sat side by side, looking out at the yard. Daisy had to admit that her friend was right. It *was* kind of pretty. The rain fell gently on the grass, leaving behind little puddles that would probably be fun to splash in later. The dark clouds had thinned out, and there was a rainbow arcing across the light gray sky.

"Wow," said Daisy in surprise.

"See?" Millie wagged her tail. "I told you so."

Daisy licked Millie's ear to say thank you and then settled down on the floor beside her friend. She wasn't sure she would ever be a fan of storms, but she knew without a doubt that she trusted Millie and was glad they were here together.

"I guess there won't be any playtime in the yard today, girls," said Danny, walking up to stand behind them. "Sorry about that."

Ron was in the next room preparing medication for Cleo, the miniature schnauzer who had an ear infection, but he looked up with concern. "I hope this rain passes soon," he said.

Danny nodded. "We'll have to prepare in

case it rains at the adoption event. But let's hope for the best. I would hate for anything to keep our pups from finding good homes." He reached down and stroked first Daisy's head, then Millie's. Then he went to assist Ron in the kitchen.

Even though they had a staff to help them run the rescue, Danny and Ron usually had plenty to do around the house. Before they'd started saving dogs together, only the two of them had lived there, and they'd spent most of their time training horses, teaching people how to ride the horses in competitions, or entertaining friends. But now they spent a lot more of their days cleaning out crates, ordering chew toys, and giving love and attention to all the dogs who lived in their home. There were so many, Ron joked that he and Danny were just guests in the dogs' house.

Daisy had been happy when she came to the rescue, and she thought it would always be her home. But Danny had said the word "adoption." She knew that meant a nice person or family would come to meet a dog, and if they liked each other, the dog would go home with them. Sometimes they'd come back to visit and tell the others all about their new lives. Danny and Ron loved to see how happy the dogs were in their forever homes.

Daisy was always thrilled for them too. But she liked her life just as it was. She whined softly.

"What's the matter now?" asked Millie. "I thought you'd gotten used to the rain."

"It isn't that," said Daisy. "Did you hear

Danny and Ron mention an adoption event?"

Millie nodded. "They usually plan them to be part of the horse shows," she answered. "But why would that worry you?"

Daisy shot a glance behind her at Ron, who was now giving Apollo his heartworm medication. He was so loving and gentle, Apollo didn't even mind. "You don't think *we'll* get adopted, do you?"

Millie scratched behind her ear with her back paw. "Don't be silly. We're not going anywhere if we don't want to," she answered. "We'll always have a home here. Danny and Ron said so."

"But what if they changed their minds?" Daisy panted, covering her snout with her paws. "If we get adopted by different families, we might never see each other again!"

"Then we'll just have to make sure that never happens," Millie said with a determined gleam in her eye. "If someone wants to adopt you, they'll have to take me too, and that's that!"

"Do you mean it?"

"Cross my paws," Millie said, which was her way of making the most serious of promises.

Daisy relaxed and went back to listening to the pitter-patter of the rain falling on the roof, and the thump of Millie's tail against the floor. She wondered, though, why Danny had touched their heads when he mentioned the event. Millie didn't seem to think that meant anything. But Daisy couldn't help thinking Danny hoped to find new homes for Daisy and Millie, too.

Chapter 2

BY THE NEXT morning, the sky had cleared, but Daisy couldn't quite shake the fear she'd felt the day before. This time, her nervous feelings had nothing to do with the weather, though.

After breakfast, while Millie took a mid-morning nap beside her, Daisy watched Danny and Ron make plans for the adoption event. They gathered the staff members and volunteers in the living room. Ron held a clipboard and a pen as he read from the list that he and Danny had written up the night before.

"As you know," Ron said, "the horse show is coming up quickly, and we would like for it to be the best adoption event ever as well. There's a lot to do, and we'll need all the help we can get. Who wants to be in charge of blowing up balloons and tying them in place?"

Right away, two hands shot up, and Ron pointed at Kim and David—college students who helped out around the rescue whenever they had time off from school.

"Great! I knew I could count on the two of you." Ron smiled and jotted down their names.

He went on, going through each of the

tasks that way. He needed people to help set up the gates outside the horse paddocks, to keep the water bowls fresh, to print out information about each of the dogs . . . the list seemed endless, but everyone was eager to pitch in.

Finally, Ron mentioned making new flyers to post around town. "We usually use pictures of the dogs being their adorable selves to promote the event. Any ideas on who should be this year's poster dogs?"

Danny gently poked Ron's arm with his elbow and jutted his chin in Daisy's and Millie's direction. "How about them?" he said. "They were among our very first rescues. I can't think of two better representatives."

Ron glanced down at Daisy and Millie and grinned. "Neither can I," he said.

As Danny took out his phone to snap some photos, Daisy pushed her snout against Millie's back. "Hey, Millie. Wake up," she whispered.

Millie yawned and mumbled, "What is it, Daisy?"

"Danny is taking our picture right now," Daisy answered.

That got Millie's attention. She rolled onto

her belly and lifted her head, just in time for Danny to take a final photo. He flipped through the images on his phone with a grin on his face. "This one will be perfect!" he declared. The photo showed Millie and Daisy with their heads pressed close together. Even though they were different breeds, the two still looked like siblings with their black fur and light spots. Millie was a whippet with white eyelashes and white spots on her muzzle and belly, while Daisy was a hound with tan patches.

After Danny walked away, Daisy turned to Millie. "They've never taken our picture for an event before. Still think it was silly of me to wonder if we're getting adopted?"

"Maybe not," Millie admitted slowly. At first, she seemed as surprised and troubled as

Daisy. But then her eyes brightened and her tail wagged.

"Why do you look so happy?" Daisy asked.

"Because being adopted could be great," answered Millie. "We could end up in a home with lots of children, or we could be adopted by a person who lives somewhere cold. We could be sled dogs! Just imagine all the fun we'd have playing in the snow."

"It won't be any fun at all if I'm there without you," Daisy answered.

Millie rested her paw on Daisy reassuringly. "I told you—I won't let that happen. Wherever you go, I go."

"But how can you guarantee that? It's not like we can tell Ron and Danny that anyone who wants to adopt one of us has to take us both. Humans don't always understand barking."

It was true. Just the other day Daisy had barked to tell Ron that she wanted ten more treats, but he had only given her one. Ron needed to brush up on his barking.

Millie nodded thoughtfully. "Then we'll find another way to show them. Don't worry.

If we get adopted, it will be together, and our new home will be somewhere we love even more than where we live now!"

"If you say so," said Daisy, trying her best to wag her tail to match Millie's. But inside she was full of doubts. How could they find anywhere better than here?

Chapter 3

LATER THAT DAY Daisy and Millie were relaxing on the couch when they heard a commotion outside. There were happy-sounding barks and people laughing.

"Why is everyone making so much *noise*?" huffed Amelia, the French bulldog who liked to spend most of her time snuggled in her bed by the fireplace.

"Elmer's here!" cried Cleo, spinning in three quick circles, the bell on her collar jingling with each turn. "He's in the backyard!"

Elmer used lived at the shelter before he'd been adopted, and everyone loved when he came back to visit. Cleo toddled through the doggy door with Apollo and Buster on her tail. To Daisy's surprise, even Amelia stirred from her nest and headed for the yard.

"Let's go!" said Millie, stretching her back. "I want to ask Elmer something. . . ." She trotted toward the doggy door and followed the others outside. Daisy padded along behind her.

In the yard, Elmer lay on his side, his fluffy black tail thumping on the grass, while the other dogs sniffed at him and yipped and yapped. "It's good to see you, Elmer," said

Buster in his deep basset hound woof.

"Thanks, Buster! It's good to see all of you, too!" He got to his paws and gave Buster a nuzzle.

Daisy had almost forgotten how cheerful and friendly Elmer could be. It had been a while since the plucky dachshund had gotten adopted by a family at a nearby military base. Benny, the little boy who had become Elmer's best friend, was watching him now from outside the fence, alongside his mother and Danny. They seemed excited to see Elmer reunite with his friends.

Millie gestured for Daisy to come closer with a tilt of her head. When she did, Millie asked Elmer, "What are you doing here? Are you only back for a visit?"

"Not exactly," Elmer said, shaking his whole body so that his long floppy ears flapped against his snout. "I've gotten pretty good at doing tricks, almost like the horses do, so a few other dogs and I will open the horse show by jumping through hoops, running between poles, and a few other things."

"Wow!" Daisy said, impressed. "I didn't know you could do all that."

"I couldn't always," Elmer answered. "But when the family that adopted me saw how fast I could run, they signed me up for classes. It was hard at first, but now I love it."

Millie wagged her tail. "So, you're glad you got adopted?"

"Yes!" Elmer yipped immediately. "Except for Danny and Ron, my new family choosing me is the best thing that ever happened to me! I have fun with them every day. They even gave me this special collar with my name and theirs on it."

"That sounds amazing," said a small voice. Daisy wasn't sure who said it at first, but then she spotted Luna, a shy white poodle, standing nearby. "I wish I had a collar like that."

"I'm sure you will one day, Luna," Elmer said encouragingly.

Just then Benny called out to Elmer.

"I have to go," Elmer panted. "But I hope I'll see you at the show!"

As Elmer yipped his goodbyes to the other dogs and rejoined his family, Millie turned to Daisy. "See? What did I tell you? Getting adopted could be great! Elmer is a star now."

Daisy scratched the ground with her paws. She had no interest in being a star. Seeing Elmer hadn't changed her mind, but she didn't have the heart to say that when Millie seemed so excited.

"I guess you're right," she said instead.

"I wonder what made Elmer's family pick him?" Millie asked.

"Well, he said they noticed he could run fast," Daisy answered. "I remember he was faster than any dog here. He could run circles around the yard in no time."

"Maybe we should try that. We need to do something that will make us both stand out and let people know we're a pair. Being the fastest dogs might help."

Daisy nodded. "All right. Let's try."

In unison, they began to trot around the yard. They went slowly at first, careful to avoid all the puddles that had been left behind by the rain, but then they picked up speed. As the other dogs outside began to blur, Daisy could feel the wind blowing past her face. Running felt pretty good. "Hey, this is fun!" she told Millie.

"Let's go faster!" Millie cried.

So they did. But soon Daisy's legs grew tired, and her mouth became dry. She could tell Millie felt the same by the way her tongue hung out of her mouth. Almost at the same time, they came to a stop, panting to catch their breath. After they drank some water, Daisy saw that Luna had been watching them run. "How many times did we make it around the yard?" she asked the poodle.

Luna looked like she was afraid to tell them. "Um . . . once?" she answered.

Millie looked surprised and disappointed. "That's it? But it felt like we were going so fast."

"Well, you were faster than the dogs who *weren't* running," said Luna, trying to be helpful.

Daisy sighed. "I don't think running is going to get us noticed."

"Maybe not," Millie admitted. "But there are other things we can try. Moose got adopted not too long ago. What did *he* do to stand out?"

Daisy thought about it. Moose was a sweet pup whose golden puffy coat had made him look like an adorable teddy bear. "He was pretty cute," she said. "I think it had to do with his fluffy hair. But that won't help us."

She and Millie had shiny hair, but it hung flat and straight, close to their bodies. And the last time either of them had been as small as Moose, they had been only months old.

But Millie smiled, her eyes bright. "I have an idea that just might work."

Daisy followed her to the edge of the yard, where a deep puddle had formed. Before she had a chance to ask Millie what they were doing there, Millie dived right into the puddle and began rolling around in the muddy water.

"Come on, roll with me!" she cried. When Daisy hesitated, she added, "Trust me."

Daisy didn't have a clue what Millie was up to, but she figured there must be a good reason for this unexpected pool party. She waded into the puddle and dunked herself in the cool water. The two of them rolled and played until their coats were soaked. When they finally climbed out, Daisy looked at Millie, confused.

"I don't get it," she said. "That was fun, but how was that supposed to make us more like Moose?"

"Just watch," said Millie. Then she shook out her coat harder than she ever had before. When she stopped, Daisy could see that Millie's coat was big and puffy, kind of like a Chow Chow's.

"Wow, it worked!" Daisy said.

"Now you give it a try," urged Millie.

Daisy did exactly what her friend had done and shook with all her might. When she

finished, she could tell by the look in Millie's eyes that she had been successful.

"Perfect!" said Millie. "Now let's go find Ron and Danny and see if they notice."

First they checked around the yard, but finding no sign of Ron and Danny there, they ducked through the doggy door and searched the house. They finally found Ron in the storage room, counting boxes of kibble. When he looked up and spotted them, he let out a hearty laugh.

"What in the world have you two gotten into now?" he said. "Look at yourselves." He pointed to a long mirror that was mounted on the wall.

Daisy was the first to look at their reflection and see that their coats were no longer big and puffy. They had settled and flattened. Now it just looked like they'd had buckets of muddy water dumped over their heads. "Oh no!" she said. "We don't look like Moose at all."

Millie whimpered. "What happened to all our beautiful fluff?"

Ron shook his head and said, "I see you've been having some fun in the puddles. Time to get you all cleaned up. Let's go see the groomers."

He led them to the back of the house where the groomers had washing stations set up with special dog shampoos, soft towels, and brushes.

"Gladys, I've got two very wet and muddy customers for you," Ron said, not bothering to hide his amusement.

Gladys and the three other groomers seemed to find the whole thing very funny too. They laughed good-naturedly, but then they got right to work. Two of them gently washed the muddy water out of Millie's coat, while the other two took care of Daisy. Most dogs didn't like taking baths, but the groomers at the rescue somehow made it fun. In no time at all, they were both clean and dry and smelled like soap.

As Daisy and Millie walked back into the house, Daisy turned to her friend and said, "Sorry that neither of those ideas worked. Maybe we should just forget about getting adopted."

"Don't give up so easily!" Millie protested. "We will find a way to make our dream come true!"

But more and more, Daisy began to realize that her dream didn't look anything like Millie's.

Chapter 4

ONE DAY AFTER the puddle mess, Millie and Daisy sat staring at a wall. But not just any wall. This one was filled with pictures of dogs. Elmer and Moose were both there, but so were lots and lots of others.

"What are we looking for again?" asked Daisy.

"These are all dogs who have been adopted," Millie explained. "Their families sent in pictures, and Danny and Ron put them up here for everyone to see. If we find other dogs who've been adopted as a pair, we can try to copy them."

"Okay," Daisy said. She studied each of the photos. The people were all different—some had long hair, some had no hair at all. Some had kids and some did not; some were young and some were old. But all the dogs looked happy and loved. Were any two dogs adopted by the same people though?

Millie let out a huff that sounded like laughter.

"What's so funny?" Daisy asked.

Millie pointed her nose at a picture of a cocker spaniel dressed as a giant sunflower. He had big yellow petals fanning out from his face and wore a green sweater that looked like a leaf. "He looks pretty silly."

Daisy glanced at the other photos again. "So does she." She pointed out a Rottweiler wearing a bright blue raincoat with a matching hat.

Millie smiled, then got a thoughtful look in her eyes. "Hey, Daisy, look at these two puppies." They were wearing matching red sweaters with reindeer on the front.

"Aw," said Daisy. "They're pretty cute."

"They're not just cute," said Millie. "They're wearing matching clothes! I bet even if they got separated, someone would know they belonged together. That's what we need to do. Find some matching outfits!"

Finally catching on, Daisy wagged her tail nervously. She had a sinking feeling what was coming next. "But where would we find that?" she asked.

"I know just the place," said Millie.

A few minutes later, Daisy found herself standing in the laundry room next to Millie. The big washing machines the staff used to

clean all the doggy beds were whirring as the loads inside tumbled in circles. And there were piles of clothes in baskets on the floor, waiting for their turn.

Daisy whined. "We're not supposed to be in here. Danny and Ron don't want us playing with the laundry."

"We aren't playing, though," Millie insisted. "We're here for a very important reason: to find matching outfits! When we do, no family will be able to resist us, and they'll know we belong together. When we get adopted, it will all be worth it."

Daisy didn't like breaking the rules, but she guessed Millie had a point. "Where should we start?" she asked.

Millie sniffed at the different baskets, then

finally stopped at the one at the end of the line. "Right here!" she said. "It's full of staff T-shirts, so they're all the same. It's perfect. Help me tip it over."

Daisy did as Millie asked and pawed one end of the basket while Millie nudged the other side with her head. Pretty soon, the T-shirts spilled out onto the floor in a great big heap.

"Good job," said Millie. "Now all we need to do is dive in and put on the shirts. How hard can it be?"

As it happened, wearing clothes was a lot harder than they thought. Daisy had never put on a T-shirt before. She didn't know which hole to put her head through. Then she got so mixed up in the jumble of shirts, she couldn't find her way out.

"Millie? Did you . . . put on a shirt yet?" Daisy cried.

"Er . . . I don't think so . . . ," Millie replied. "How about you?"

"I . . . I might be just a little bit . . . stuck," Daisy answered. But the truth was, she was a *lot* stuck. Her back paw poked through the arm holes of one T-shirt, another one had knotted around her front paws, and her head hadn't quite pushed through the neck of a third, which now draped over her head like a shower curtain.

That's when Daisy heard Ron's deep voice say, "What have you two gotten yourselves into now?"

It took a few minutes for Ron and Danny to untangle Daisy and Millie from the staff shirts. But before they freed the dogs completely, Ron lifted his phone to take a picture. *Flash!*

"Well? What do you have to say for yourselves?" he asked, looking at the photo he'd just taken and then back at them.

Daisy, who still had a T-shirt hanging off her right ear, thought about diving back into the pile of shirts. She had no answer to Ron's question, and neither did Millie, who still had a

T-shirt wound around her back left paw.

"They know better than to play in the laundry room. What were they thinking?" Danny wondered out loud.

"I don't know," answered Ron. "But this does give me an idea. It might be nice to have some of the dogs wearing Danny & Ron's Rescue gear at the adoption event."

"Just maybe not on their heads," Danny added. He lifted the T-shirt dangling from Daisy's ear and chuckled.

"Right," Ron agreed. "And since we don't have time to get T-shirts made to fit the dogs, maybe we can alter some of these shirts and turn them into bandanas. They clearly want to wear them." He pointed at the dogs with his thumb.

"Great idea," Danny said. "The photographer we hired can get shots of them in the bandanas for our website."

"That sounds perfect." Ron turned back toward Millie and Daisy and squatted down so that he was at eye level with them. "As for you two, we don't want to catch you playing around in here again. Understand?"

All Daisy knew was that Ron's calm voice and the amused twinkle in his eyes meant that she and Millie were forgiven. Daisy hurried forward and licked Ron's cheek. Millie did the same thing on the other side. They were so grateful, they nearly knocked him over.

"All right, all right," he said, laughing. "Go on now."

Millie and Daisy filed out of the laundry room and settled down by the fireplace next to a few other dogs. Daisy let out a deep sigh.

"Where have you two been?" asked Buster in his slow howl.

Millie quickly explained what happened in the laundry room, and Amelia yipped at them right away.

"What in the world made you think causing trouble was the right thing to do?" she asked.

"It seemed like a good idea at the time," said Millie. "If matching shirts won't get us adopted together, I'm not sure what will."

"Is that what you thought?" Buster's eyes drooped even more than usual. "That's not going to work."

"Then what is the secret?" Millie asked, her tail wagging hopefully.

"There *is* no secret," Buster said. "You just

have to find the right family. You'll know it when you meet them."

Daisy thought that sounded wise. Maybe they didn't have to worry about this as much as they had been. If the perfect family was out there, they would find her and Millie.

"Thanks for the good advice, Buster," said Millie. But as she snuggled in close to Daisy, she whispered, "I still think there's a way for us to make our dream come true. Maybe if I sleep on it, it will come to me."

Daisy waited until Millie's breathing became deep and even, and her paws began to twitch like they always did when Millie dreamed about running. Then Daisy slowly got to her paws and slipped outside on her own. She needed to think too.

Chapter 5

WHEN DAISY NEEDED time alone, the horse stables were her favorite place to go. She loved the smell of the hay and the soft neighing of the horses. Plus, sometimes she would find bits of apples on the ground. But today, she wasn't the only dog who had come looking for peace and quiet.

At the end of the row of stalls, Luna sat stiffly

on her haunches near Sable, a horse who had come to live at the rescue after being found at an abandoned farm. Sable was still recovering, but doing much better than before. She had gained weight and her mane was bright and full. Luna, on the other paw, looked like she had just lost her best friend. Daisy could tell by Luna's hunched shoulders and dry nose that something was wrong.

"What's the matter, Luna?" Daisy asked as she got closer.

Luna looked up at Daisy, her dark eyes full of sadness. "It's nothing," she said. "You'll think I'm being silly."

"I'm sure that isn't true," Daisy replied. "You can tell me. We're all friends here."

Luna looked at Sable, who twitched her ears.

"It's just . . . ," Luna began slowly, "I'm afraid that I'm so shy, I'll never be adopted. Every time we have an adoption event, I get all excited, but then I end up hiding so that no one can see me."

Daisy was stunned. She'd been so wrapped up in her own problems, she hadn't noticed that her friend Luna had problems of her own.

"You're worried about the adoption event too?" Daisy asked. "I thought I was the only one."

"You?" said Luna, looking surprised. "But why would you be worried? You aren't shy like I am."

Daisy nodded. "That's true. But I do get scared easily. Danny and Ron's house is the only place I've ever felt safe, and I don't really want to leave."

"Who says you have to?" asked Luna.

"Well, Danny and Ron have been dropping hints. And Millie *wants* to get adopted. But I'm not sure, and I'm afraid if I tell Millie that, it will hurt her feelings. After all, we do everything together, and adoption is her dream. So I've just been going along with it."

Luna scooted closer. "You have to be honest with Millie. Adoption might be the right thing for her, but it's okay if it's not right for you." Sable neighed then, swishing her tail and lightly brushing at the hay beneath her hooves.

Daisy sighed. "You might be right. I don't want to be separated from Millie, but even more than that, I don't want to keep her from finding a family."

"Even if you aren't together, you'll always be friends," Luna noted.

"That's true. Maybe if Millie is adopted, she can come back to visit like Elmer does." Daisy thought for a moment, then said, "And Luna, I don't think you need to worry about the event."

"Why's that?" Luna tilted her head quizzically.

"Buster said that when you find the right family, you'll know it. Maybe when you meet the right people, you won't feel so shy around them."

"Maybe. Thanks, Daisy, for listening."

Daisy wished Luna goodnight then headed back toward the house. On the way, she thought about their conversation. She knew in her heart that she wanted to stay at the rescue, but if she told Millie, her friend might be angry or might feel like she had to stay too. Although Millie was usually the one with all the brilliant plans, this time Daisy would have to come up with one of her own. She just hoped she had the nerve to go through with it.

Chapter 6

BRIGHT AND EARLY in the morning, after all the dogs had eaten breakfast and had a good stretch, Danny let them out into the yard to play. This was usually one of Daisy's favorite times of the day. She loved when she and Millie chased each other around the grassy field, or when they lay side by side and scratched their backs on the ground while looking up at the clouds. She especially liked tugging on opposite ends of the same rope. Millie made every day fun.

But not today. Today Daisy vowed to stay as far away from her best friend as she could.

While Millie stopped for a drink of water, Daisy trotted over to the other side of the yard and pretended to be very interested in chewing on a stick. Eventually, Millie came over, her tail wagging and her ears at attention.

"Hey, Daisy, want to play? Kim just put some new toys out."

Daisy desperately wanted to play with Millie. But she shook her head. "No. I don't want to." She looked around the yard at the other dogs. Buster seemed to be having fun chas-

ing his own tail. "I think I'll go play with Buster instead," she announced.

Daisy hurried away, but not before she saw the confused look in Millie's eyes. Daisy felt terrible about deserting her friend. *But this is all part of the plan,* she reminded herself. *I'm doing this for Millie's own good.*

At first Buster seemed just as confused as

Millie had when Daisy asked him if she could play. But he welcomed the help in chasing his tail. For some reason, it was hard to do on his own. Even when Daisy started to get dizzy, she kept running in circles, right up until Millie came over to try to get her attention again.

"Can I play too?" Millie asked politely.

"Sure," said Buster. "Between the three of us, we're sure to catch my tail!"

But Daisy was already backing away. "I'm pretty tired of playing," she said. "But you two have fun."

With that, Daisy walked away. She spotted Laura rounding the yard to clean up behind the dogs and decided to follow her. Maybe if she looked busy helping a staff member work, Millie would stay away.

"Hey, Daisy!" said Laura brightly as Daisy padded over. Laura gave her a quick scratch behind both ears before saying, "Where's your friend Millie?"

Daisy couldn't help glancing back across the yard, where she'd left Millie chasing Buster's tail. But now Millie was standing still, staring at Daisy, looking lost. It seemed like she had finally gotten the hint that Daisy wanted to be left alone. Daisy's plan was working. She should have felt good, but instead she felt worse than ever.

"Taking a little time apart, huh?" said Laura. "Well, that's all right. Do you want to keep me company instead?"

Daisy barked once before rubbing her broad head against Laura's knee.

"I'll take that as a yes," said Laura.

For the next fifteen minutes, Daisy walked alongside Laura as she refilled water bowls, plucked weeds out of the grass, and gathered up stray toys that needed to be washed. It wasn't as fun as playing with Millie, but she did like the way Laura talked to her the whole time she went about her tasks. It was just what she needed to take her mind off the fact that her plan to make Millie think they weren't friends anymore was working. Maybe now Millie would feel okay about getting adopted without her.

The day went by slowly. Without Millie to talk to, Daisy didn't know quite what to do with herself. She napped, she visited Sable, and she wandered around the house. But all that was only enough to fill a couple hours. She was glad when a truck pulled up to the house and provided a new distraction.

Daisy watched through an open window as Ron and Danny greeted the driver out front. Together, the three of them pulled boxes out of the back of the truck. Inside were more supplies for the adoption event, which was only a few days away.

After the driver left, Ron opened one of the boxes to reveal a stack of connected gates. They unfolded into a basic square shape with a door on one side. Danny opened a second box to reveal an already assembled doghouse. It looked exactly like Danny and Ron's rescue—only smaller.

"It's perfect!" Danny exclaimed, moving the doghouse into the center of the square. "A dog or two can rest inside if it gets too hot."

"Or if it rains," added Ron. "I'm still not sure if the storm heading down the coast will land here or not."

"Well, if it does, we'll be ready," said Danny. "For now, we should see if these gates will work for the stars of our show. I'll be back with a few volunteers."

Daisy didn't know that by "volunteers" he meant dogs until he came bounding into the house to scoop up Luna. She may have been nervous around most people, but not Danny. She relaxed against his shoulder, while he scanned the room.

"That's one," he said. "I need two more."

When he spotted Millie just inside the dining room, he called her forward. "Millie the T-shirt Bandit makes two. Now, where's your partner in laundry crime?"

Daisy knew he meant her. She tried to burrow into the couch cushions, but she could only hide her front half. Her other half was sticking out in the open. Danny patted her back gently and said, "You're number three, Daisy. Come on out."

Daisy slowly climbed down from the couch and followed Millie, Luna, and Danny out to the front yard. Ron smiled as Danny ushered Daisy and Millie through the open door of the gates, then set Luna down between them.

"If these three like it," he said, "I think the gates will work great for the adoption event."

Daisy was glad Danny had chosen Luna to be one of the volunteers. Not only had Luna proven to be a good friend, but with her around, Daisy could avoid Millie for just a little while longer. Every time Millie tried to get close to talk to her, Daisy moved closer to Luna. She stuck to the poodle as she investigated, sniffing at the gates and poking her head into the doghouse.

"Oooh," Luna howled into the empty space. She smiled with her tongue hanging out. "I bet when dogs are adopted, they get a doghouse just like this one to sleep in."

"Yeah, maybe . . . ," Daisy said.

"Pretty soon we'll get to meet all the people who want to take a dog home. Maybe they'll want one just like me!" Luna continued.

As Luna went on and on, happily picturing the families who would come to the event, Daisy became more and more over-whelmed. It was all too much. She always knew when a storm was coming because the air would smell different, and her hair would stand up on end. She felt the same way now about the adoption event. All she wanted to do was hide. But since she didn't have her blanket, she scurried into the small doghouse and settled down in the shade.

Millie poked her nose in curiously. "Daisy, are you okay?"

But Daisy quickly closed her eyes and pre-tended to be asleep. She even added in some loud snoring sounds. Millie crept closer and sniffed at Daisy, but still, she didn't stir.

The next thing Daisy heard was Millie

barking and pawing at the gate. "Ron, come quick!" she called. "Something's wrong with Daisy!"

Ron, who had been standing outside the enclosure chatting with Danny, came over to see what all the fuss was about.

"What happened, Millie? Did you see a squirrel?"

But Millie ran back to the doghouse and barked and barked. Daisy eased one eye open long enough to see Millie looking from Ron to the doghouse and back again. That's all it took to put him on high alert. He hurried inside the gate then peered down at Daisy.

"Is everything all right?" Danny asked.

"I'm not sure," answered Ron, reaching into the doghouse to stroke Daisy's head. "She has been sleeping a lot today. More than usual. And it's clear that Millie thinks something is wrong."

Then Danny said the words that made Daisy realize she had played this all wrong: "Maybe it's time to take her to the vet."

Chapter 7

A COUPLE OF DAYS had passed since Daisy's trip to the vet. It hadn't been as bad as she'd feared. Dr. Kim and her staff were kind, and since Daisy was an older dog, they pulled out all the stops. They weighed her, examined her teeth, and listened to her heart. They checked her skin to make sure it wasn't too oily or too dry. They ran lots of tests. But Daisy already knew that no test would find what had really been troubling her: She liked her life just as it was and didn't want it to change.

That's the thought that was running through Daisy's mind when Danny and Ron came into the mudroom that morning. They had set her up in a crate away from the other animals until they could be sure she had a clean bill of health. They checked on her often, but this time they weren't alone.

"We weren't expecting a house call, Dr. Kim," Danny said. "I hope that doesn't mean you have bad news about Daisy's test results."

"Not at all," said Dr. Kim as she walked in and settled into a chair facing Daisy's crate. "I'm here because I wanted to check in on some other patients of mine in your care, as well as Daisy. But the news for her is good. According to all my tests, Daisy's health is just fine. If anything, I did notice the other day that the muscles in her hind legs were a bit tight. Has she been unusually active lately?"

"Hmm . . . ," Ron said, scrunching up his brow as he thought. "Well, I did see her running around the yard with Millie a few days ago. They were both moving faster than they normally do."

"And there was the whole T-shirt incident," added Ron. The two of them explained how they'd found Daisy and Millie all tangled up in a pile of staff T-shirts. At the time, Daisy had been worried that she and Millie might never free themselves from the mountain of cotton. But now, when she thought about that day, all she could remember was having fun with her best friend.

Dr. Kim nodded and let out a short laugh. "That could be it. I think Daisy just tired herself out. As an older dog, she needs plenty of exercise, but she also needs plenty of rest. Otherwise, though, Daisy is clear to rejoin the other dogs."

"Thank you, Dr. Kim," Danny said, squatting so he could smile at Daisy. "That's a relief to hear, huh, girl?"

Daisy panted happily.

"I assure you," he continued, facing the doctor, "for the rest of the day, Daisy is going to be the most pampered pooch in the house."

Danny's words came true. That afternoon, Daisy felt like she lived in a luxurious doggy day spa. First, she visited the groomers, who gave her coat a long, luxurious brush until it was soft and shiny, and they gently trimmed her nails. Then Ron revealed that he'd gotten Daisy a new bed, especially made for older dogs. When she lay down on it, Daisy felt like she was sleeping on a cloud. The best part was when Danny settled in next to her bed to rub her belly until she began to drift off.

But as much as she loved all the pampering and attention, she felt guilty, too. Everyone had been scared that she was sick, when really, she had just been worrying herself into knots.

As soon as Danny got up to help Ron get dinner ready for the dogs, Millie hurried over to Daisy. She sniffed at her friend and licked her ear. "Hi, Daisy," she said, seeming hesitant. "How are you feeling?"

"I'm fine," said Daisy. "It's good to see you."

Millie looked surprised and relieved. "It is?" she said. "The way you acted before you went to see the doctor, well . . . I thought maybe you were mad at me or something."

Daisy lowered her head sorrowfully. Her plan hadn't been such a good idea after all, and she didn't want to hurt Millie's feelings any-more. "I was never mad at you," she said. "I'm sorry I made you think so."

Millie shook it off quickly, her eyes bright-ening instantly. "That's all right. I'm just glad we're friends again!" she cried. "Because tomorrow is the big day, and I'm going to need you by my side."

Big day? Daisy thought, confused. Then she remembered: The adoption event was finally here. Between the visit to the vet and her day of pampering, she'd nearly forgotten.

Millie climbed into the big comfy dog bed next to Daisy and snuggled up to her. "Tomorrow will be so much fun," she gushed. "And who knows? Maybe we'll meet our forever family there."

Daisy didn't have the heart to tell Millie that she hoped she was wrong.

Chapter 8

BRIGHT AND EARLY the next morning, the house bustled with activity. Volunteers gathered carrying cases for the smaller dogs, and safety harnesses for the larger ones. Danny and Ron scurried around, making sure they had enough food and water. And outside, a large bus idled, waiting to take them all to the horse show and adoption event.

"Have we got everything?" Ron asked Danny.

"I think so," he said.

"Then let's load up the dogs and hit the road!"

Daisy found herself riding in the bus filled with dogs, and she sat near Millie, Cleo, Luna, and a Labradoodle who had arrived at the rescue just that week. The horse show was being held at an arena about an hour away from their home, so Daisy had plenty of time to gaze out the window. The sun shone brightly, and the sky looked clear and blue, but Daisy couldn't shake the feeling that it wouldn't stay that way.

An hour later, the bus pulled into the arena, where the horse show would soon begin. Hundreds of people were already filling up the stands surrounding the main exhibit area. But outside, a large clearing had been reserved just for Danny & Ron's Rescue.

In no time at all, the team unpacked the bus and got ready for the adoption event. Danny and Ron put up the enclosures for the dogs, while the other staff members unfolded the information table, blew up balloons, and set up tents. Others took boxes into a nearby barn. Danny and Ron kept making sure the staff knew no one was allowed into the barn yet—not even the dogs. But Daisy figured that was only because they were keeping extra food and toys in there and didn't want them to get distracted. Finally, Danny came to lead Millie and Daisy into one of the enclosures along with the small, empty doghouse. But just before he ushered them inside, he pulled two brightly colored bandanas out of his pocket.

"We had these made just for you," he announced proudly.

Quickly, he fastened the bandanas, first around Millie's neck, then Daisy's. They were perfect fits.

"How do we look?" asked Millie, wagging her tail extra hard.

The bandanas were just like the yellow staff T-shirts (without the pesky armholes) and had the rescue's logo right on the front—a red heart with a dog print in the corner.

"We look adorable," Daisy admitted.

"What a pretty girl!" said a familiar voice. Daisy looked up just in time to see Ron hug a slender woman with short gray hair and red eyeglasses. She wore a light green track-suit and sneakers, and Daisy knew who she was right away. She was the trainer who had worked with Daisy when they'd first come to live at the rescue.

"Eileen!" Ron greeted her warmly. "I'm so glad you could make it."

"Me too," Eileen replied. "It's good to see you, and Daisy, of course. How are all the dogs doing?"

Oh no. Daisy felt her belly rumble with dread while Ron showed Eileen around and chatted about the event. The last time she'd seen Eileen, she was there to help Daisy settle in to her new home and get over her fears. *She must be here because she knows I'm about to be adopted into another new home!* Daisy thought.

And as Daisy watched the adoption event begin to take shape and people start to wander in, she felt the buzzing in the air that let her know a storm was coming. Suddenly Daisy wished she had brought her favorite blanket, or that she could run back home. She longed to be close to the bed she used to hide under. When Daisy let out a soft whine, Millie glanced at her with concern.

"Is everything all right, Daisy?" she asked.

Daisy fought the urge to say, *No! Nothing is all right! Can't you tell a storm is coming?* Instead, she shook out her coat, let out a yawn, and said, "Everything's fine."

"Great!" said Millie. "Because I see lots of nice people here who could use a couple of dogs like us to help eat their peanut butter and chew on their slippers."

Millie turned and lifted herself onto her back legs, pressed her front paws against the fence, and wagged her tail. In moments, a young boy had spotted Millie.

"Mom, look at this one!" he said, pointing at her. He grabbed his mother's hand and dragged her over.

"Oh, she's good," Luna whispered to

Daisy. "I wish I were as outgoing as Millie."

Daisy wanted to reassure the shy poodle, tell her that she could do anything she set her mind to. But all her focus was on trying to keep herself calm.

Millie craned her head back and called, "Daisy, come over here and meet this family. We have to show them we're a team, remember?"

Daisy remembered. So why couldn't she stop backing away?

Ron walked over then, a smile lighting up his face. "I see you've found a few of our favorite rescue dogs," he said. He reached out and gave Millie a scratch behind her ear.

"Yes, they're so beautiful," said the woman. "Are they all available for adoption?"

Danny, who had just opened the door to the enclosure to refill their water bowl, said, "Actually, they—" But that was as far as he got, because just then a shadow fell over the grounds and a loud *boom* sounded in the sky.

Ron looked up and held out his hand, palm up. "Oh no. Is that what I think it is?"

"It's raining!" someone yelled.

Then a bolt of lightning flashed against

the darkening clouds, and suddenly Daisy was racing through the open gate.

"Daisy, wait!" Millie called out. But Daisy couldn't stop her legs from pumping. She sped right past Danny, past a table full of flyers about the dogs, past the group of kids huddled under one of the tents . . . and straight into the forbidden barn.

Chapter 9

DAISY COULDN'T SEE anything inside the quiet barn. The door had swung shut again behind her, and there were no lights on. Even if there had been, it wouldn't have mattered. She had buried herself beneath a pile of fresh hay and curled up into a ball. As hiding places go, the barn wasn't quite as good as her blanket or her spot under the bed

back home, but it would do for now.

The barn door inched open with a creak. Just enough that Daisy could hear the rain falling heavily outside. This was no gentle pitter-patter like before. She knew that if she were to peek out, she wouldn't see a rainbow, but dark rain clouds, sheets of water falling from the sky, and people running for cover.

"Daisy? Are you in here?"

Daisy recognized Millie's bark. She must have seen Daisy run into the barn and had come looking for her.

"No," she answered.

A minute later, she felt the straw around her stir as Millie came sniffing. She got closer and closer, until Daisy could feel Millie's wet nose on her snout. "Ah, there you are," Millie said. "Are you okay?"

Daisy shook her head, sending pieces of golden hay falling into the soft piles around her. "Of course not," she said. "How could I be? Didn't you hear that thunder? Did you see the light-ning? I knew a storm was coming. I just knew it!"

"You're right," Millie agreed. "It's raining pretty hard outside right now. But is that really what's got your fur in a bunch?"

"What do you mean?" asked Daisy.

Millie let out a slow huff. "Well, even before it started raining, you seemed . . . nervous."

Daisy slumped. Millie knew her too well.

"The truth is," Daisy began, "I don't want to get adopted!" she finally blurted out. It felt good to get that off her chest at last.

"You don't? Why didn't you tell me?" Millie asked.

"Because getting adopted is your dream!" cried Daisy. "You can't wait to find a forever family, and I didn't want to ruin it for you. So I pretended to be excited too. But then Luna said that what's right for each of us might be different choices. I knew that was true—that's why I stopped hanging out with you, so you could be adopted without me. But I still didn't want that to happen, and I didn't want to go anyplace new, either. For a while, it all seemed so far away. But then we got here, and all these people crowded around us, and that woman and her son asked if we were available for adoption . . . it was all too much."

"And then it started raining," Millie filled in.

"Right," said Daisy. "So, I ran away."

Daisy felt sure that Millie would be upset with her for hiding the truth for so long, and for being such a scaredy cat. It surprised her when Millie snuggled in close to Daisy instead and said, "I'm so sorry."

Daisy lifted her head, confused. "You are? What for?"

"I thought getting adopted would be a dream for both of us. I'm sorry I didn't know how you felt. It's all right if you like things the way they are."

"Thanks, Millie," Daisy said, feeling under-stood for the first time all week. "Some things will change though when you find your for-ever family."

"Daisy, *you* are a part of my forever family," Millie replied. "Being with you is more impor-tant to me than being adopted."

Feeling overwhelmed with happiness, Daisy shut her eyes and pressed her head against Millie's.

"If you don't want to get adopted, what *do* you want?" Millie asked.

Daisy didn't have to think long. "I want us both to stay at the rescue with Danny and Ron. But now it might be too late!"

"What makes you say that?" asked Millie.

Daisy pointed out how Danny had touched their heads when talking about finding homes for their pups, and the trouble they'd gone to in order to make them the bandanas. "He even brought Eileen here!" she finished. "The only reason my old trainer would be here is to help me settle into a new home!"

Millie let a low rumble sound in her throat. "When you put it all together like that . . . ," she said. "Maybe you're right."

But before either of them had the chance to be sad about it, the barn door swung open, someone flicked a switch, and suddenly, the room was filled with light.

"Come on inside, everyone!" Ron called out.

As crowds of people moved into the barn,

and the Rescue staff brought in the dogs from the other enclosures, Danny spotted Millie and Daisy, still half buried in hay.

"There you two are!" he said. He clapped his hands together happily, then came to kneel by their side. "Well, it looks like you both discovered the little surprise party we had planned for you ahead of time. Oh well. You might as well come on out and enjoy it now!"

Daisy glanced at Millie. "What's a surprise party?"

"Let's go find out!" Millie replied.

Slowly the two dogs climbed out of the haystack they'd huddled in together, and they walked into the clearing in the middle of the room. Daisy couldn't believe her eyes. Instead of a storage space, the barn looked more like doggy heaven. In one corner there were piles of brand-new toys. Plush toys and squeaky toys, and ropes and tennis balls and Frisbees. In another corner were bags of all their favorite treats, and what looked like cupcakes for dogs. In the middle were big oversized fluffy beds, and bowls of fresh water. Above it all was a banner stretching from one side of the rafters to the other with another sign on the wall beneath it. They said:

HAPPY GOTCHA DAY, DAISY AND MILLIE!

FROM YOUR FUREVER FAMILY AT DANNY & RON'S RESCUE

"Is this really all for us?" Daisy asked.

"I think so," said Millie. "Look." She used her snout to point at a few poster-size photos that had been taped to the barn walls. One was of

Millie and Daisy cuddled up by the fireplace. Another was of the two of them in the laundry room, tangled up in T-shirts. And the last was of Millie and Daisy right after they'd been rescued from Louisiana.

After the people had finished piling into the barn and closed the door firmly behind them, Ron and Danny made their way to the front of the room, where someone had built a makeshift stage.

Ron's deep voice called out, "If I could have everyone's attention . . ."

Slowly, the chatter in the room died down and all eyes turned to Ron.

"Thank you for coming to today's adoption event," he said. "It turned out to be soggier than we'd hoped, but we're not going to let a little rain stop us from showing these amazing dogs some love, are we?"

The crowd clapped and cheered. And the other dogs, who were now roaming freely around the barn, wagged their tails.

Danny added, "When we first started taking in dogs who needed our help after Hurricane Katrina, we had no idea what an adventure we were in for. But here we are several years and thousands of dogs later, and we wouldn't have it any other way."

Ron nodded. "Some of you have been lucky enough to be adopted by one of our dogs."

Everyone laughed. Daisy spotted Elmer and his family near the front of the room. The little boy, Benny, held Elmer in his arms and gave him a cuddle.

"But some very special dogs become permanent members of *our* family," said Danny. "And we wanted to celebrate two of our forever canine family members right now."

With that, Danny kneeled down and looked right at Daisy and Millie. "Come here, girls," he said, waving them forward. He blew them a few quick air-kisses and patted his thigh.

Daisy padded along next to Millie as they joined Danny on the stage. He gave each of them a treat then turned back to the crowd. "Daisy and Milly here were two of the very first dogs we ever rescued. Because of what they went through, Daisy did have some struggles to work through. Thank you, Eileen, for helping us out with her."

Eileen raised her hand and smiled. "My pleasure."

"But we realized that the best thing for Daisy was to keep her life stable and never make her leave a home she loved again. She and her best friend, Millie, will always have a home with us. So, when you support our work by adopting a dog, or by donating to the rescue, know that you are making it possible for us to guarantee any dog who comes through our doors has a home for life if they need it."

"Does he really mean that?" asked Daisy.

"Can't you see?" Millie replied.

Daisy followed Millie's gaze as she looked out at the crowd. She saw Gladys and the staff of groomers, the college volunteers, Dr. Kim, Eileen the trainer, and even Luna peeking her tiny nose out from behind the pile of toys. And of course, Danny and Ron stood behind them like proud parents.

"We didn't have to try to find a forever family . . . ," Millie began.

"Because we already have one," Daisy finished.

She realized she had been worried over nothing. She and Millie had been adopted by Danny and Ron, and everyone at the rescue. Suddenly the rain outside didn't seem so bad. In fact, everything seemed as bright as a rainbow.

Chapter 10

FOR THE NEXT hour, Daisy didn't worry about storms or adoptions or her blanket being far, far away. She didn't even try to hide under anything, not even once.

Instead, she just had fun.

She and Millie ran around with Elmer, scarfed up doggy cupcakes, and tried out all the new dog toys. Her favorites were the kind that squeaked or lit up when she chewed on them. She jumped onto bales of hay and met all the nice people who had come in search of a dog to take home. She was enjoying a belly rub from one woman with curly gray hair and a pretty pearl necklace when the woman called Ron over.

"Are you sure this one isn't available for adoption?" the woman asked Ron, gesturing to Daisy.

Ron smiled and shook his head. "I'm sorry, but we simply couldn't run the rescue without Daisy and Millie. They're our favorite mascots. But I hope you'll consider one of other dogs."

The woman nodded but didn't seem convinced.

For the first time that day, Daisy had a very

good idea. She rolled onto her paws and went to find Millie, who was happily gnawing on a bully stick.

"Millie," she called. "I need your help."

Millie looked up from her stick. She looked curious. "Don't tell me you changed your mind and want to get adopted now."

"No," Daisy answered quickly. "But there's another dog here who does, but she's going to need a nudge. And who comes up with better plans than us?"

Millie grinned. "No one, that's who!"

Daisy wiggled her pointy ears. "Right! So, it's time for step one of the plan: Find Luna!"

Daisy and Millie may not have been as fast as Elmer or as fluffy as Moose, but no one had better sniffers. The two of them used their powerful noses as they made their way around the barn. It wasn't long before Daisy's nose led her right to a trembling pile of hay. It was the same spot she had hidden in when she first ran into the barn.

"Luna, is that you under there?" she asked.

"M-maybe," said Luna.

Millie, swiped away some pieces of hay with her heavy paws, and soon they could see their curly-headed friend. "Why are you hiding?" Millie asked. "I thought you wanted to get adopted?"

Luna cast her eyes down. "I d-do," she stammered.

"But no one can see you hiding here under the hay," Daisy pointed out.

"I know. But I can't help it. I'm just too shy."

"That's why we're here," said Daisy. She quickly told Luna about step two of her plan. The two of them would walk on either side of Luna as they introduced her to someone that they thought she should meet.

"And you won't leave my side?" Luna asked.

"Not until you're okay on your own," Daisy promised. She and Millie crossed their paws.

It took a little time, but finally Daisy and Millie coaxed Luna out of her hiding place and into the party. As soon as Daisy spotted the kind woman who gave her the belly rub, she steered Luna right in her direction and bumped into her knees.

"Oh!" the woman called in surprise. But when she glanced down, she saw three sets of hopeful eyes pointing her way. "Well, what do we have here?" she exclaimed.

"Now's your chance, Luna," said Daisy, nudging her forward the slightest bit.

Luna wiggled her stubby tail nervously, and the woman said. "Aww. Aren't you adorable!" She reached out and stroked Luna's head. Instantly, the poodle relaxed. Soon, the woman was talking and cooing to Luna, and

Luna was brave enough to let her.

Daisy and Millie inched away little by little.

"It's like they belong together!" Daisy said.

"They even have the same hairstyle," Millie agreed.

And as the party began to wrap up, Daisy was pleased to hear the woman call Ron over and tell him that she had fallen head over heels in love with Luna.

Ron smiled down at Luna, and asked, "What do you think, girl? Would you like to go home with her?"

Luna let out an enthusiastic, "Yes!" It was

the loudest sound Daisy had ever heard her make. Ron and the woman laughed.

"We just helped make a forever family," Millie said.

Daisy beamed with pride. Ron had been right. This was the best adoption event ever.

One month later, Daisy and Millie were cuddling by the fireplace, keeping Amelia company. Since the adoption event, everything had gone back to normal. Buster chased his tail, Amelia complained about the noise, new puppies made messes on the floor, Danny and Ron buzzed around like busy bees . . . and Daisy and Millie remained the best of friends. Only one thing at the rescue had changed.

Luna was gone.

Not long after the adoption event, the woman who'd fallen in love with the once-shy poodle came to officially make Luna part of her family. Daisy had been sad to see her go, but she was happy for her friend.

Millie had just stretched and let out a yawn when Danny came striding into the room, holding a stack of mail. He sifted through the pile until he came across a light blue envelope. He opened the flap and pulled out a festive-looking card with the words THANK YOU! on the front. Danny flipped it open and read the letter aloud.

Dear Danny and Ron,
Thank you for introducing me to my new best friend, Luna. We're having the best time together, and it turns

out she loves to go for long bike rides with me. If it wasn't for your rescue, we never would have found each other. Here's a picture of us for your wall.

Your friend,

Sandy

Danny held up a glossy photo and said, "What do you say, girls? Want to come with me to add a picture to our Hall of Fame?"

He didn't have to ask twice. Daisy and Millie trotted along behind Danny as he made his way toward the wall. He reached for a tack and pushed it through the photo. When he backed up, Daisy finally saw Luna in her new home. Only, Luna was peering out from a wicker basket fastened to the handlebars of a bicycle. Sandy's smiling face was pictured right above the poodle's, and they were wearing matching helmets. Luna looked happier than ever.

Daisy was thrilled that Luna had found her forever home.

And with Millie, Danny, and Ron by her side, Daisy had too.

Danny & Ron's Rescue is a real place in South Carolina. Both professional horse trainers, Danny Robertshaw and Ron Danta have been rescuing dogs ever since 2005, when they started helping animals in Louisiana in the wake of Hurricane Katrina. But they didn't stop there. Soon they opened their hearts and home to dogs who had suffered in puppy mills and dog fights, who lived in shelters and junkyards, or who had been abandoned and were living on the streets. With assistance from a hardworking staff including veterinarians and groomers, the dogs in their care are spayed or neutered, vaccinated, dewormed, groomed, and microchipped.

Danny & Ron's Rescue is one of the only organizations that does not charge a pre-set adoption fee, but instead requests an affordable donation from the adopter. But what makes the rescue truly unique is that the dogs live in Danny and Ron's actual house and often sleep in the bed. At any time, they have as many as eighty-six dogs inside with an additional thirty-five to forty dogs on the farm. There are so many more dogs than humans there now that Danny and Ron consider themselves guests in the dogs' house.

What was once a quiet home for two, including their horse stables, is now a safe haven for dogs who have been injured, abused, or neglected. There, not only do they receive organic food and a warm place to sleep, but they are loved and treated like part of the family until they are adopted by a family all their own. Since the founding of their rescue, Danny and Ron have homed more than thirteen thousand dogs.

But some very special dogs find a permanent home with Danny and Ron, often because they are too ill to be adopted out, or because they have experienced something traumatic and the best thing for them is to remain at the rescue.

Daisy and Millie were two of the dogs rescued from the floods in Louisiana during Hurricane Katrina. It is not known exactly what became of their original owners, but many people were forced to abandon their pets when they were evacuated from the area. Others passed away, leaving their pets to await rescue on the porches and roofs of their homes. Organizations including the ASPCA, the Humane Society of the United States, Best Friends Animal Society, and Animal Rescue New Orleans (ARNO) worked tirelessly to save these animals and reunite them with their loved ones. But the task was daunting, as some 250,000 animals had been left behind. The trauma caused by forcing humans to abandon their animals

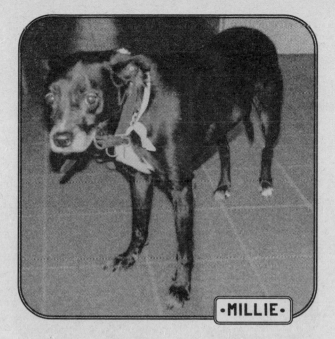

·MILLIE·

led directly to the passing of the Pets Evac-
uation and Transportation Standards Act in
2006. From then on, rescue agencies would
be required to save animals as well as people
when terrible natural disasters occur.

Danny and Ron found Daisy and Millie
among the thousands of rescued dogs who
were brought to local shelters. The two were

·DAISY·

so tightly bonded that they were inseparable. Danny and Ron soon realized that not only could the dogs never be parted from each other, but they would need to be permanent residents of Danny & Ron's Rescue. Both dogs are so sweet and good-natured that they have never regretted this decision for a moment.

In the story, a trainer named Eileen Clark helps Daisy overcome her fear of storms. While the trainer is fictional, she is named for two real people. Eileen Danta, Ron Danta's mother, passed away in 2019, but the fund established in her honor lives on. Mom's Fund is dedicated to helping rescued dogs get lifesaving surgeries. Missy Clark is the founder of the Dandelion Fund Medical Assistance Program, which provides financial assistance for dogs with life-threatening medical conditions.

Life in the Doghouse, the documentary about Danny & Ron's Rescue, is available on most major streaming platforms. The film details how the rescue came to be, shows the challenges of running the twenty-two-acre farm, and highlights some of the special dogs that have called it home over the years. Since its debut, *Life in the Doghouse* has won the title of Best Full-Length Documentary at the Tryon International Film Festival in 2018, and it was an official selection of the Frameline San Francisco International LGBT Film Festival, the Provincetown Film Festival, and Newport Film. It has been profiled on everything from the *CBS Evening News* to the *Today Show* and the Hallmark Channel.

If you would like to find out more about Danny & Ron's Rescue and how you can help dogs like Daisy and Millie, visit their website at dannyronsrescue.org, or learn more about the documentary at LifeInTheDoghouseMovie.com.

Turn the page for a sneak peek of

Elmer's Life in the Doghouse!

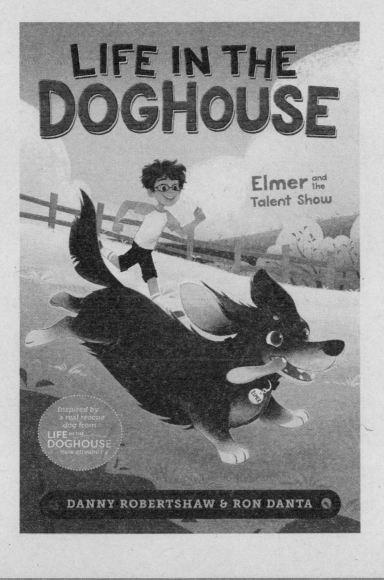

ELMER LOVED LOTS of things—belly rubs, ear scratches, squishy toys that squeaked when he chewed on them. But his favorite was definitely hearing the *scoop, scoop* sound that meant Danny and Ron, the humans who ran the dog rescue where he lived, were awake and making breakfast.

"Good morning, Elmer!" Danny unlatched

Elmer's crate and put a silver bowl filled with food inside. Elmer gave Danny's hand a quick lick and wagged his tail before he started eating. "Aw, I love you, too," Danny said.

Buster, the brown-and-white basset hound with the droopy eyes, was still snoring away in a bed by the fireplace. But most of the others stirred the moment the light in the kitchen blinked on. Elmer could hear Lucy's high-pitched yip from the crate above his and Momo's satisfied snuffles and grunts from the end of the hallway. Elmer wasn't the only one who loved digging in to the feast every morning, but he was one of the few who had to have special food that was soft and easy to chew.

After breakfast Danny opened the dogs' crates and led them to the backyard.

"All right, go play!" he said, his grin crinkling the corners of his blue eyes.

Elmer didn't hesitate. He liked showing Danny and Ron how good he was at running across the fresh green grass, with his long hair blowing in the wind. On his little dachshund legs, he could run even faster than Joey, the Jack Russell terrier.

Elmer trotted around the large yard, stopping only long enough to sniff Charlie the Chihuahua and bat a lime-green tennis ball with his paws. All the playing made him thirsty. Most days were pretty sunny and hot in South Carolina, but Danny and Ron made sure the dogs had lots of shady spots to rest and plenty to drink. Elmer padded over to one of the bowls of water that were tucked against the side of the redbrick house. After lapping up a few sips, he peered down into the bowl. When the ripples stilled, he could see his own reflection in the water. He had been born with a misshapen mouth that made it hard to eat, and not long ago, he could barely see out of his right eye. It took six surgeries and weeks of wearing a cone around his neck, but the doctors had fixed his jaw and saved his eye. His lips no longer closed, he was missing teeth, and his long tongue hung from the side of his mouth. But he had survived.

Ron and Danny told Elmer all the time that he was a good boy, a beautiful dog who would find his forever home any day now. But when he looked at himself, he wasn't so sure. After all, why would anyone adopt him when they could take home Lady, the adorable gold-colored corgi, or the litter of five-month-old German shepherds—Huey, Dewey, and Louie—who were so tiny when they first got to the rescue that they had to be fed with a baby bottle? People usually wanted the puppies—or at least cute dogs who didn't need surgery just to straighten their snout.

But Elmer tried not to let that get him down. He knew he was lucky to be with Danny and Ron. After all, not many horse trainers would turn their own home into a dog rescue, but years ago, that's just what they did. When they weren't teaching riders how to lead horses through a series of jumps during competitions, they started helping dogs who needed them. At first they saved just a few pups who had lost their homes in a hurricane and were all alone in the world. Danny and Ron set aside space for the dogs in their horse stables, then nursed them back to health, and found them loving families. But soon the numbers grew and grew, and the horse stables weren't enough. So their dining room table became rows of crates. Instead of stacking logs in their fireplace, they filled it with dog beds, and stocked their pantry with kibble. Eventually, their house had more dogs than people. They often said that they were only guests now in the dogs' house.

Elmer loved life at the rescue. There were always lots of pups—and sometimes cats—to play with, nobody minded if he jumped up on the sofa in the living room, and when it rained outside and he got scared, Danny would sit beside him and stroke his long soft ears until he fell asleep. Like most of the animals in the house, Elmer remembered what it was like to live in a place where he wasn't safe. Here, Elmer knew he would be taken care of, no matter what. Still, that didn't change the fact that his dearest wish in the world was for some nice people to take him home and make him part of their family.

He lay on his back, cushioned by the soft grass, imagining what that would be like. As he looked up at the fluffy white clouds drifting across the sky, Elmer heard the rumble of a car approaching the house. He rolled onto his belly and watched the apple-red sedan wind down the path and come to a stop near the fenced-in yard. Soon Ron came out into the sun, lifting his hand in greeting, a wide grin on his face. "You must be the Cruz family," he said.

The man behind the wheel opened his car door and stepped out, nodding his head. As tall as Ron, he had tan skin and a trimmed beard that covered his cheeks and chin, but didn't hide his bright smile.

"We are," the man answered, shaking Ron's hand. "I'm Reggie, and this is my wife, Sergeant Cruz." He gestured toward a woman in a green-and-tan army uniform coming around the front of the car. Her jet-black hair was pulled into a tight bun, and she had warm hazel eyes and deep dimples when she smiled.

"You can call me Marisol," she said. "And this is our son, Benicio. . . ." She looked behind her to find no one there. She sighed. "Benny, come on out and say hello."

That's when Elmer noticed the young boy

sitting in the back seat of the car with his nose pressed up against the window. His dark, wavy hair stuck out in all different directions, and behind his glasses his wide eyes were almost the same brown as Elmer's paws. He was nervously biting the corner of his lip as he finally pushed open his door and climbed out of the car. "Hi," he mumbled quietly, and waved before shoving his hands back into his pockets.

"Hello there," Ron said. Then he turned to Marisol and whispered, "He isn't scared of dogs, is he?"

Marisol shook her head. "No, he's actually really excited to be here. He's just a little shy with new people. It's one of the reasons we want to adopt a dog. Reggie and I are used to moving every few years, whenever the military reassigns me. But I'm afraid it's been kind of tough on Benny."

"We thought maybe if he had someone to keep him company, that might help," Reggie added. "And nothing makes it easier to meet new friends than a cute puppy, am I right?"

"I can't argue with you there," Ron answered. "Why don't you come inside so you can fill out some paperwork. And Benny?" he said, looking down at the boy, who had nestled against his mom's hip. "If you want, you can stay here and watch the dogs play. It might help you decide what kind you'd like. Just stay outside the gate, all right?"

"I'll keep an eye on him," said Laura, one of the staff members, as she tossed a few more toys into the yard.

After Benny glanced at his mom and dad to make sure it was okay, he grinned and ran right up to the enclosure, peering through the fence.

Elmer couldn't explain why—maybe it was the excited look on the boy's face, or the fact that Benny seemed to need someone just as much as he did—but Elmer wanted this family to adopt him even more than he wanted a chew toy filled with peanut butter. And that was saying a lot!

Elmer trotted over and lifted his front paws onto the fence, letting out a series of yips that meant *Hi! I'm Elmer. Want to play?*

Benny did look down at him, and even stuck his fingers through the fence to boop the tip of his nose. But it wasn't long before his eyes wandered to the side of Elmer's face where his taffy pink tongue poked through. Elmer's wounds had healed, but he knew some people thought he wasn't as cute as the other dogs, and he wasn't as young as the puppies. In human years, he was only ten years old, but in dog years, he was seventy, a senior. So, it came as no surprise that Benny's eyes lit up when Huey, Dewey, and Louie came barreling toward the gate. The boy didn't even notice when Elmer offered him his paw to shake or when he bounced around in a circle, letting his ears flap like bird wings. *He wants a cute little puppy,* Elmer thought. His tail drooped.

Just then, the door of the house opened, and Ron led Reggie and Marisol outside.

"Well, Benny?" Marisol said as she joined her son by the gate. "See any dogs you like?"

Benny nodded and pointed at the German shepherd pups.

"Good choice," Ron said. "German shepherds are great with kids. These are already spoken for, but we do have a new litter that just arrived a few weeks ago. They still need to pass a few medical checks, but I can add you to the adoption waitlist."

"Thanks," said Reggie, resting his hand on Benny's shoulder. "We'll look forward to hearing from you."

With that, the family climbed back into the red car and drove away.

Elmer watched as the Cruz family sped down the road, and Benny turned in his seat to stare out the rear window and smile. For just a moment, Elmer let himself believe that Benny was smiling at him.

DANNY ROBERTSHAW and **RON DANTA** are horse trainers and animal lovers who began helping dogs way before 2005. But when Hurricane Katrina hit, their rescue began in earnest as they saved over six hundred dogs from that national disaster. For their work during Katrina, they were 2008 ASPCA Honorees of the Year. Since then, Danny and Ron have used their personal home for Danny & Ron's Rescue, formed as a nonprofit 501(c)(3) that has saved over thirteen thousand dogs, all placed in loving homes. Danny, Ron, and their rescue were the subjects of the award-winning documentary *Life in the Doghouse*. They have also been featured on the *Today* show, *CBS Evening News*, the Hallmark Channel, *Pickler & Ben*, and several other TV shows. Their mission is a lifetime promise of love and care to every dog they take in. Visit them @DannyRonsRescue and at DannyRonsRescue.org, and learn more at LifeInTheDoghouseMovie.com.

CRYSTAL VELASQUEZ is the author of several books for children, including the

American Girl: Forever Friends series, the graphic novel *Just Princesses*, the Hunters of Chaos series, the Your Life, but . . . series, and four books in the Maya & Miguel series. Her short story "Guillermina" is featured in Edgardo Miranda-Rodriguez's anthology *Ricanstruction: Reminiscing and Rebuilding Puerto Rico*. She holds a BA in creative writing from Penn State University and is a graduate of NYU's Summer Publishing Institute. Currently an editor at Working Partners Ltd., she lives in Flushing, Queens, in New York City and is the go-to dog sitter for all her friends. Visit her website at CrystalVelasquez.com, or follow her at Facebook.com/CrystalVelasquezAuthor or @CrystalVelasquezAuthor on Instagram.

LAURA CATRINELLA is an illustrator and character designer who loves to play with shapes and colors. She has fun creating a variety of different characters and people, all while being able to play around and tell a story with them. Usually, she can be found drawing at a park or coffee shop. Laura resides in British Columbia, Canada, and she spends most (all) of her time with her two mini dachshunds, Peanut and Timmy.

READ & LEARN

with

simon kids

Keep your child reading, learning,
and having fun with Simon Kids!

A one-stop shop where you can
**find downloadable resources, watch interactive author
videos, browse books by reading level, and more!**

Visit us at
SimonandSchusterPublishing.com/ReadandLearn/

And follow us @SimonKids

75458

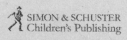

SIMON & SCHUSTER
Children's Publishing